W9-BHA-998

The World's Birthday

A ROSH HASHANAH STORY

Barbara Diamond Goldin

PICTURES BY **Jeanette Winter**

HARCOURT CHILDREN'S BOOKS
HOUGHTON MIFFLIN HARCOURT
BOSTON NEW YORK 2009

Text copyright © 1990 by Barbara Diamond Goldin
Illustrations copyright © 1990 by Jeanette Winter

All rights reserved. No part of this publication may be
reproduced or transmitted in any form or by any means,
electronic or mechanical, including photocopy, recording,
or any information storage and retrieval system, without
permission in writing from the publisher.

For information about permission to reproduce selections
from this book, write to:
Permissions
Houghton Mifflin Harcourt Publishing Company
215 Park Avenue South
New York, NY 10003

www.hmhbooks.com

Library of Congress Cataloging-in-Publication Data
is on file.

The quotation on the facing page is from the Rabbinical
Assembly *Mahzor for Rosh Hashanah and Yom Kippur*, p. 267.

The illustrations were done in Winsor & Newton and
Holbein watercolors on Strathmore Bristol 3-ply paper.
The display type was set in Lucian Bold, by Latent
Lettering, New York, New York.
The text type was set in Garamond No. 3 by Thompson
Type, San Diego, California.
Color separations were made by Bright Arts, Ltd., Hong
Kong.
Printed and bound by Tien Wah Press, Singapore
Edited by Jane Yolen and designed by Joy Chu
Hardcover ISBN: 0-15-299648-6

This edition published specially for The Harold
Grinspoon Foundation © 2009 by Houghton Mifflin
Harcourt Publishing Company.

Special Markets ISBN: 978-0-547-25942-0

For Alan
— B.D. G.

To Mr. Jacobson
—J.W.

Zeh hayom tekhilat maasekha zeecaron l'yom reeshon.

This day is the birthday of Creation,
a reminder of the first day.

Daniel loved Rosh Hashanah. He would wear his new clothes for the holiday. On the way to synagogue, he would step on the fallen leaves, *crunch*, *crunch*. He could almost hear the sound of the shofar, the horn the cantor blew, calling, "Wake up! Wake up!" Best of all, everyone in his neighborhood would stop to wish him a good New Year.

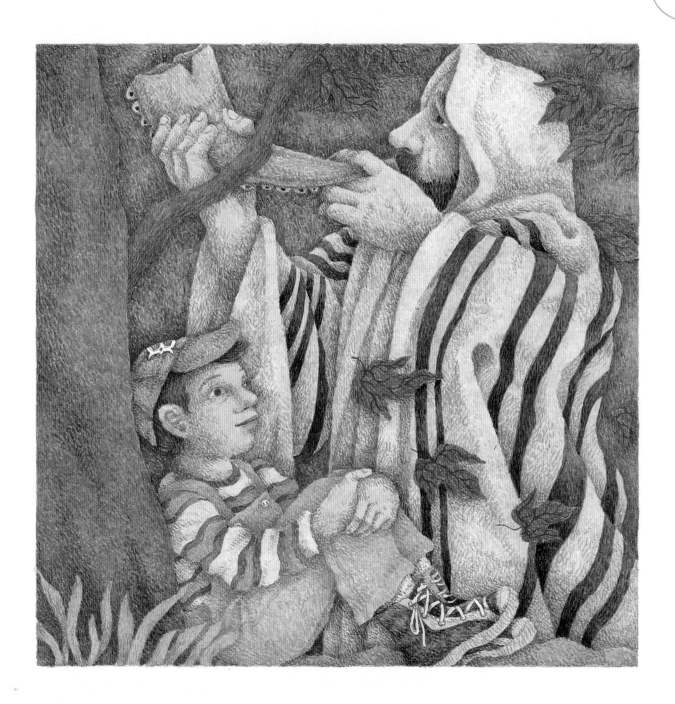

"How many more days until Rosh Hashanah?" Daniel asked his Papa one bedtime. He knew it was soon. Mama was already mixing the dough for the round, braided egg breads, the "challahs."

"Two more days," his Papa answered. "Now come to bed. You, too," he called to Daniel's sisters, Leah and Naomi.

"Why do I have to go to bed when they do?" complained Naomi. "I'm the oldest."

"Because I only have time for one bedtime story," said Papa. "What'll it be?"

"Tell us one about Rosh Hashanah," said Daniel. "I know the Purim story and the Passover story and —"

"I know that one," Naomi interrupted. "Rosh Hashanah is the world's birthday."

"You're right," Papa said. "On Rosh Hashanah we celebrate the time when God created all things."

"On my birthday I have a party," said Daniel. "Could we have a party for the world?"

"But what would you do at a party like that?" asked Papa.

"I would have a cake and burn candles and invite the whole world."

"Please — me, too," said little Leah.

"Of course you, too," said Daniel. He pulled affectionately on Leah's blankie. "Could we have such a party, Papa?"

"A party for the world's birthday? What a stupid idea," said Naomi.

"Talk to me tomorrow," said Papa.

The next day, Daniel hadn't forgotten the birthday of the world.

"Mama," he asked, "can we go to the bakery so I can buy the biggest cake Mr. Gutman has for Rosh Hashanah?"

"Why do you want to buy a cake, Daniel?" Mama asked. "Naomi and I are making those nice honey cakes."

"It's for the world's birthday," Daniel told her.

"But you can't have a party for the world," said Naomi disgustedly. "It's much too big to fit into our house."

Daniel looked all around the house: in the kitchen, in the living room, in the bedrooms. Even in the bath. There was not enough room for the world. Maybe Naomi was right.

"I know," Daniel said, "I'll ask Mr. Gutman. He knows all about parties and birthday cakes."

Naomi walked Daniel to the bakery. She shook her head at him at every other step. But Daniel didn't notice. He bought the biggest cake in the bakery window with the money Mama had given him. Mr. Gutman gave him a few pennies' change.

"It's for a party for the world," he told Mr. Gutman. "Rosh Hashanah is the world's birthday."

"In all the years I've been selling challahs and honey cakes for Rosh Hashanah, I never knew that," said the baker. "How do you make a party for the world?"

"I was going to ask you that," said Daniel.

"Maybe you should ask your grandfather instead," said Mr. Gutman. "He's a rabbi. *He* would know, if anyone does."

"I will," said Daniel. "But please, Mr. Gutman, will you come to my party?"

"Don't worry, I'll come," said Mr. Gutman. "Maybe you'll want some candles before you go? For the birthday cake?"

"Oh, I forgot," said Daniel. He counted out his pennies. "One, two, three."

"You don't even have enough for one box," said Naomi.

"Here, take four boxes," said Mr. Gutman. "It's on me. After all, the world is no young chicken."

"Thank you," said Daniel.

Daniel and Naomi put the boxes of candles in their pockets and together carried the cake down the street to Grandpa's house. They knocked on his door.

"Grandpa," said Daniel, "since it's Rosh Hashanah and Rosh Hashanah is the world's birthday, I want to make a birthday party for the world. Have you ever seen a party for the whole world?"

"No," said Grandpa. "I've never heard of anyone making a birthday party for the world. Isn't the world too big to come to a party?"

"See? I told you so," said Naomi.

Grandpa looked thoughtful. "There *is* something you could do."

"What, Grandpa?"

"On Rosh Hashanah, people like to make cards for each other and wish each other a good New Year. Maybe you could make a card for the world and wish for a good New Year for everyone and everything."

"But the party tonight . . ."

"Don't worry," said Grandpa. Gently he touched Daniel's shoulder. "I'll come tonight. You can show me the card then."

"I will, Grandpa," Daniel said.

He and Naomi walked back to their house, Daniel carefully carrying the cake.

"Now what are we going to do with it?" asked Naomi.

"We'll still have the party," said Daniel.

Naomi put her hand on her hip. "You can't do that. You can't have the party without the guest of honor."

"Don't worry," answered Daniel.

After supper, Daniel began to work on the card. As he drew, he remembered the story Papa had told him of how God created the world. Of how God made darkness and light first, then the sky and the land and all the other things.

Daniel drew the stars, the sun, and the moon in his pictures. He made fish, birds, animals, and people.

When he finished his drawing, he thought about his mother giving him the money for the cake. He thought about the baker and the boxes of candles. He thought about his grandfather and the card with all the things that God had created. Suddenly he knew how he could have a party for the whole world.

That night, Mr. Gutman and Grandpa came to Daniel's house.

Daniel led them all outside—Mama, Papa, Leah, Naomi, Mr. Gutman, and Grandpa.

"Why are we going outside?" Naomi asked.

"You'll see," Daniel answered.

He walked in front of them carrying the big birthday cake into the night, close to the sky and the trees and the grass and the animals and the whole world.

He put the cake down on the grass and reached into his pocket for the candles. He began to place them on the cake.

Naomi was the first to understand. "I guess you *can* have a party for the world," she said. "Let me help you."

"Thanks," said Daniel.

When they finished, Mama lit the candles.

"So many," Leah said.

"That's because the world is so old," answered Daniel.

The candles blazed against the darkness.

"Let's sing 'Happy Birthday, World,'" Daniel said.

They sang, and Daniel sang loudest of all.

Just as they finished the song, a strong breeze came along. *Whoosh.* It blew out all the candles.

Daniel looked up at the sky and smiled. "I hope you remembered to make a wish first," he said.

Rosh Hashanah is Hebrew for "head of the year" or "New Year." One of the holiest of all Jewish holidays, Rosh Hashanah is celebrated in the fall. It is a time of deep reflection and soul-searching, when Jews customarily ask forgiveness from any person they may have wronged over the past year. On Rosh Hashanah itself, Jews also go to synagogue to ask forgiveness from God.

Rosh Hashanah has other names as well. One is *Yom Teru'ah*, "Day of the Shofar," for the ram's horn or shofar that is blown at synagogue calling: "Wake up! What have you been doing? What will you do in the New Year?"

Another name for the holiday is *Yom Harat Olam*, or "The Day of the Birth of the World," commemorating the sixth day of creation, when God made man and woman and completed the physical creation of the world.